COWBOY JESS

Also by Geraldine McCaughrean

Cowboy Jess Saddles Up

Great Stories from British History

George and the Dragon and a
World of Other Stories

King Arthur and a World of Other Stories

Robin Hood and the Golden Arrow and a
World of Other Stories

Stories from Shakespeare

COWBOY JESS

Geraldine McCaughrean

Orion
Children's Books

First published in Great Britain in 1995
by Orion Children's Books
a division of the Orion Publishing Group Ltd
Orion House
5 Upper St Martin's Lane
London WC2H 9EA
An Hachette UK company

This edition first published in 2011

1 3 5 7 9 10 8 6 4 2

Text copyright © Geraldine McCaughrean 1995, 2011
Illustrations copyright © Tavis Coburn 2011

A catalogue record for this book is available from the British Library.

ISBN 978 1 85881 291 5

Printed in Great Britain

The Orion Publishing Group's policy is to use papers that are natural,
renewable and recyclable products made from wood grown in sustainable
forests. The logging and manufacturing processes are expected to
conform to the environmental regulations of the country of origin.

www.orionbooks.co.uk

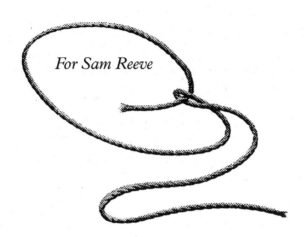

For Sam Reeve

Contents

1 ★   **Jess Ford**   1

2 ★   **Wanted**   5

3 ★   **Sweet Rain**   21

4 ★   **The Noon Stage**   35

5 ★   **The Army Brand**   49

6 ★   **The Christmas Mittens**   61

1

Jess Ford

No one quite knew where Jess Ford had sprung
from. That is to say, they knew where they had
found him, but not the reason for him being there
or where he rightly should have been at the time.
He was found as a baby, sleeping soundly inside a
raccoon hat. One cold spring morning a cowboy
out rounding up strays found him, between the
tracks of four wagon wheels, by a burned-out
campfire, beside the Sweetwater River crossing. It
was just as if he'd been overlooked and left behind.
The raccoon fur was all spangled with dew, like
diamonds, but the only other riches found on this
particular wayfarer were a brass pocket watch and
two lead pencils.

People reckoned he was an orphan even before he got mislaid, 'cos no one came back looking for him, and even the most absent-minded mothers and fathers generally notice losing a thing like a child. They called him *Jess*, after the cowboy who found him, and *Ford* after the place where he got found.

Sundown was real new in those days, not settled yet, and not what the County Judge called 'a suitable environment for a newborn person'. Everyone who lived there had come from some place else – no one had been born there. (You might say Jess was the first native-born Sundowner.) And everyone was pretty busy doing whatever they came to Sundown to do – homesteading, ranching, dancing, keeping the peace. Still, they were kind-hearted folk, and took it in turns to look after the raccoon-baby, all the time thinking someone would come by and claim him.

The dancing girls at the Silver Dollar Saloon kept him in their dressing room, sleeping him in a hat box with purple stripes. The storekeeper's wife cleared a space among the haberdashery and slept him on a pile of starchy pillowcases. The blacksmith slept him in a manger near the furnace – till the preacher's wife protested fiercely that it was NO place for a baby and said she had never heard the like.

The bartender slept Jess in a beer crate. He spent a night or two in the Sheriff's jail (when it wasn't otherwise occupied), and the Widow Bramley took him for a while. But she wasn't a widow in those days, and Mr Bramley couldn't *stand* the smell of babies, so Jess had to go.

All in all, Jess Ford kinda belonged to everyone and to no one. He was truly a son of Sundown, and everyone had a soft spot for him. As Jess grew up, so did Sundown.

The preacher's wife said the pencils found on the baby proved he was the son of educated folk. So Sheriff Sparrow taught him to read. When he had managed it, the preacher's wife folded her hands proudly over her stomach and said, 'There. I said it was in his blood to be eddercated.' Sheriff Sparrow just growled like a bear.

Given his beginnings, Jess grew up quite ordinary. His hair was reddish and his face was frecklish and his legs were longish for his size – like on a young horse. It's true, he did choose to sleep out under the stars whenever he could, but then that's only natural in a boy born on a wagon trail and cradled in a raccoon hat.

And of course he hadn't a red cent to call his own. So he started working just as soon as anyone would pay him to sweep a yard or weed a vegetable patch. Kitchen work was best: there were always free meals to be had. But what Jess wanted – what Jess wanted more than meat or drink or money – was to be a cowboy. In his heart of hearts, he did not believe life would really begin till he swung his leg over a saddle and rode out on to the range, a lariat on his thigh. Sometimes he wished he could have slept the years away, curled up inside that raccoon hat, and not come out at all till someone shook his shoulder and shouted in his ear, 'Ride 'em out, Cowboy Jess!'

2
Wanted

Sheriff Sparrow tacked the notice on to the trunk of the big old hickory tree. It said:

> **WANTED**
> **Red-neck Pete, for horse rustling.**
> **$50 Reward.**

He nailed it right alongside another notice on the tree:

> **WANTED**
> **COWHANDS. DOLLAR A DAY AND KEEP.**
> **APPLY LAZY J RANCH.**

The Sheriff stood back to see if his notice was straight.

'I'm going after that money,' said Herbert from the bank, and he fetched his horse from the livery stable and bought beans from the grocery store, for his journey.

'Fifty bucks, eh?' said Pat Bodger from the saloon bar, and he crammed on his hat, drank two fingers of rye, and mounted up.

'That money's for me,' said Regan, checking both his guns were fully loaded.

They peered hard at the picture on the Sheriff's poster, a black-haired, thin-faced man with a moustache perched on his lip thin as a stem of liquorice. Then they rode out of the town three different ways.

Jess Ford stood looking at the tree. 'I'm going after that money,' he said, and walked out of Sundown, all the way to the Lazy J Ranch.

'I've come after the job, sir,' he told the ramrod, the foreman in charge of the ranch hands.

'Where's your horse, son?' asked the ramrod, polishing a bridle in his lap.

'Don't have a horse, sir, but I reckon if I work hard and save . . .'

'Never heard of a cowboy without a horse,' said the ramrod. 'Never heard of one, and I'm not about to hire one. Sorry, son.'

Jess bit his lip and pushed his thumbs deeper into his belt. 'But I have to be a cowboy. I never wanted anything else.'

'You don't want the cows stomping on you. So go home. A cowboy needs a horse. Go home.' Jess turned to go, his shoulders drooping, head down. The ramrod's blue eyes watched him out of a face wrinkled like leather. He was a hard man, but his heart was as soft as saddle soap. 'Think you can feed some chickens and a hog or two?' he called after Jess.

'Sure!'

'Caint pay a dollar a day, but you could have your keep, and a bed in the bunkhouse. The hands might teach you a bit about working horses and cattle.'

'That would be swell!' cried Jess, and shook the man's hand before he could change his mind.

So Jess Ford went to work at the Lazy J Ranch. In the morning he fed the chickens, hunted out the eggs they laid, and took them to the cookhouse.

'That boy has a nose for eggs,' said the cook.

'He can find them even in the dangdest places.'

Jess fed the pigs and scratched their backs with a stick, then he swept the yard, weeded the farmhouse garden and oiled the wheels of the buggy. He changed the hay in the bunkhouse and shook out the blankets. Sometimes the rancher, Bossman J, gave him notices to paint – *KEEP OFF: PRIVATE PROPERTY* or *NO TRESPASSING* – because Jess had been to school and could read and write.

'Danged if that boy don't spell better than I do,' said Bossman J.

When the cowhands rode in weary at suppertime, they let Jess unsaddle and water their horses. Sometimes they even let him practise with their lariat ropes, lassoing the fence post. If he got up early he could go and hang over the stable door talking to Bossman J's own saddle horses – the palomino and the grey. Everyone knew Bossman J rode and bred the best saddle horses in the county.

He got no pay. After a week, he was not one cent richer. Jess did not see how he would ever save up to get himself a horse. But he was happy at the Lazy J. When he bedded down at night on the straw bales, and the cowboys were snoring all around, he could shut his eyes and feel like one of them.

★ ★ ★

Meanwhile, Herbert from the bank was out looking for Red-neck Pete, the horse thief. With that fifty dollar reward he could ask Minnie Good to marry him.

He rode up to Deadend Canyon; he figured that was a good place to hide stolen horses. The canyon was so deep that the sun never shone on its scrubby floor. There were dark cracks in the cliffs, high, thin waterfalls and half-a-hundred caves. Herbert had a little silver pocket pistol with him. Minnie had loaned it to him. He checked that the gun was loaded and climbed to the mouth of the nearest cave. He could hear something moving about inside! But it was very dark. So he struck a match against a rock. A big shadow leapt up the cave wall – the shadow of a man!

Herbert was so scared by his own shadow that he clenched both fists tight. The match burned him, and the little pocket pistol went off. The bang rang through the cave so loud that Herbert thought his ears would drop off. Then a shape came at him out of the dark.

A big old bear, alarmed by the noise, came wading out of the cave. Herbert threw his gun at its nose and ran. He ran till both heels fell off his new cowboy boots. He startled his horse, and she bolted. Herbert hung on to her tail all the way to the brink of the canyon.

Back in Sundown, at the Silver Dollar Saloon, Herbert ordered three glasses of rye and drank them straight down.

'Well? Did you ketch Red-neck Pete?' asked the bartender.

'I had him! I cornered him up at Deadend Canyon. *Stop right there,* I told him, *or I'll blast you!*'

'Oh, Herbert, did you really?' cried Minnie.

'But he came out shooting, and a lucky bullet knocked the pistol out of my hand. Then the cave roof fell in on him and blocked the entrance. There was nothing I could do but head back home.

'You mean you lost my gun?' said Minnie.

'What about the horses? Did you see my stolen horses?' said Bossman J.

'What happened to your boots?' asked the bartender.

'Herbert! You've been drinking!' said Minnie. 'I can smell it!' Then she flounced out of the saloon.

★ ★ ★

Pat Bodger went up to the old abandoned silver mine. He figured that was a good place to hide stolen horses. He took a bottle of whisky with him, to pass the time, and he settled down to watch the mine entrance. He rested his rifle on a rock and looked along its sights. The moment Red-neck Pete showed himself – PYOW! Pat would collect the reward. He could not see any horses: perhaps they were hidden in the mine, too.

The sun was hot. Pat had a drink, then he had another. The whisky made him thirsty, so he had a third. Red-neck Pete did not come out of the cave all morning. Pat tilted his hat forward to rest his poor eyes from the glare . . .

When he woke up, three hours later, there was a rattlesnake coiled up on his chest. His bottle of rye had fallen over, and the snake was drinking the spill, licking it up with a flickering tongue. Pat lay very, *very* still. It seemed like he lay still for a winter and two Christmases. Finally, the snake stopped sipping. It had no eyelids; how could he tell if it was asleep? At last it fell off his chest, with a noise like a baby dropping its rattle. Its coils fell, *flip*, *flop*, across his rifle.

Pat crawled away so carefully that he wore the knees out of his trousers. He crawled right under his horse, and she trod on him. Then he rode like calamity for the far horizon.

Back at the Silver Dollar Saloon, he asked for a glass of water and a damp cloth to put on his aching head.

'Well? Did you ketch Red-neck Pete?' asked the bartender.

'I had him in my sights. Indeed I did! *Put your hands in the air and step forwards real slow*, I said. Then the mouth of the mine suddenly collapsed – those timbers must be rotten as rotten – and all I could see was a cloud of dust.'

'Seems like we had an earthquake hereabouts today,' said the bartender. 'And to think I never noticed it.'

'What about the horses? Did you see my stolen horses?' asked Bossman J.

'What happened to your trousers?' said Belle, the dancer.

'Where's your rifle?' asked the Sheriff.

Before Pat could answer, the saloon doors flapped, and in came Regan with his hat on back to front.

'Well, did *you* ketch Red-neck Pete?' asked the bartender.

'I did! I would have! I had him tied up and slung over his saddle, and I was bringing him in! But his whole gang jumped me. There must have been twenty of them, and they came at me guns blazing. I tried to fight them off, but there were just too many. I had to let Pete's horse go in the end, to save my skin.'

'Did you happen to see my stolen horses?' asked Bossman J.

'Er . . . They ran off,' said Regan hurriedly, turning rather red.

'In the earthquake, I suppose,' muttered the bartender under his breath.

★ ★ ★

'What does it mean, sir?' asked Jess, wiping his paintbrush on a rag. *KEEP OUT – LOCO BRONCO*, said the notice at his feet. 'What does "loco bronco" mean?'

'It means, boy, that I spent a whole hatful of money buying me a horse, and the brute turns out to be a killer. A black mare. She looks as pretty as the Rocky Mountains – she's about as tall – and she runs like a river. But she's plumb star-gazing mad. I was robbed. She won't carry a rider, won't even carry a saddle. And she's dangerous. I've shut her up in the dark. But if I can't break her spirit, I'll just have to shoot her. She's a demon, and that's a fact. Now you fix that notice to the loose-box door, so no one goes near and gets hurt. Then you can muck out the stable. Mrs J and I are going to town.'

There was no noise from the loose-box, as Jess nailed up the notice: *KEEP OUT – LOCO BRONCO*. As tall and pretty as the Rocky Mountains? He just had to see. Jess loved horses better than Sundays. So he waited till the rancher and his wife had driven away in the buggy. Then he shot the bolt on the loose-box door and opened it just a crack.

The sun stabbed the inner dark like a sword. It shone in the eyes of the horse inside. Her eyes rolled, her nostrils flared, and she leapt at the door, baring her teeth. When Jess pushed the door shut, in the nick of time, the horse threw out her heels and kicked at the back wall till it seemed the whole building would fall apart. Planks splintered. The wet new notice fell off the door, its fresh paint face-down in the dirt. The pigs started squealing. The hens scuttled into the barn.

Sick with sorrow, Jess tried to get on with his work. He picked up the rake and went to the stable, to drag the dirty straw out into the yard. But he found the door of the grey horse's stall was already open. A man stood beside the grey, his hand on its bridle: a black-haired, thin-faced man in a red bandanna, with a moustache like a stem of liquorice. As Jess entered, the man half drew a gun from under the flap of his long cloth jacket.

They looked at one another across the shifting back of the restless mare.

'Guess you've come to see Bossman J,' said Jess.

The man looked puzzled, flustered, then his face brightened. 'Yeah! Sure! That's it.'

'He'll be back pretty soon. I expect you came about the horses.'

'What horses?' said the man. 'Yeah. Yeah. About the horses.'

'Bossman said he was thinking of selling,' said Jess. 'You must want to buy.'

15

'That's me. I'm buying. That's me.'

'Well, if you want my advice, that's not the best of them, you know. The best is the black.'

The man's eyes bulged a little with glee. 'Is that a fact? Well, why don't you show me this black. I might be interested.' The gun slipped back into its holster. A cunning smirk twisted the mouth beneath the thin black moustache.

Jess led the way. He shot the bolts on the loose-box door and opened it just wide enough for the stranger to slip inside. Then he shut it again. Fast. He picked up the notice lying face down in the dirt. *KEEP OUT – LOCO BRONCO.* He would have to paint it again.

By this time, the stranger was beating on the door with both fists. 'Let me out! This horse is trying to kill me! What's the big idea?'

'Throw your gun out under the door, Red-neck Pete,' said Jess. 'The game's up.'

A six-gun came skidding under the door. 'Now open up, boy!'

'Throw out your boots, now, Red-neck Pete,' said Jess. Angry hooves cracked at the loose-box wall. 'And now your trousers.'

'You satisfied yet? Let me outa here!'

'I might. If you tell me where the stolen horses are, Red-neck Pete,' said Jess coolly.

'On injun land! Blind Canyon! On the reservation! Okay? Now, please! This fiend's eaten my jacket!'

As Bossman J drove the buggy into the front yard, his wife gave a shriek and covered her eyes. 'J! There's a man with no trousers tied to our porch!'

Jess Ford raised his hat politely to Mrs J. Then he said, 'Your stolen horses are in Blind Canyon on the Indian reservation, sir. This here is Red-neck Pete. Ramrod's gone to fetch the Sheriff.'

★ ★ ★

Sheriff Sparrow counted the reward money into Jess's hand. 'Forty-eight, forty-nine, fifty.' Everyone in the Silver Dollar Saloon clapped and cheered. 'And what do you plan doing with such riches, Mr Ford?' he asked.

'I'm fixing to buy a horse, sir,' said Jess.

'You should get a fine beast for the money.'

But Jess put his head on one side and shrugged in the strangest way.

'Nope. I reckon I must be born to go on foot.'

He took the money straight back to the Lazy J, and laid it down in front of Bossman J. 'Will that buy the loco bronco, sir?'

Bossman gaped at him. 'That'll buy you the best quarterhorse this side of the state line! What do you want with that witch?'

'I can't bear to see her shot, sir,' said Jess. 'I'd sooner turn her loose on the range.'

Slowly, coin by coin, Bossman J picked up the shiny dollars. 'Well, she's yours now, boy. So you'd best be the one who lets her go. But stand well clear, or she may stomp you into the dirt.'

Jess Ford went out to the loose-box and drew back the bolts. 'You're free, lady,' he whispered, and swung the door wide.

The horse which bolted past him was black as thunderclouds with a streaming silken mane and coal-black tail. She pelted across the yard, through the orchard and jumped a post-and-rail fence. She galloped up the hill to where a mesquite tree cast a single spiky shadow, and there she reared up and blew through her nostrils, pawing the ground with her hooves. Her ears swivelled, listening to every

sound off the open range. Then she trotted a way
back down the hill, her eyes fixed on Jess.

They met halfway, as a cowboy and his horse
should: halfway between the hill and the ranch
house. Jess put a hand on her neck and the mare
nuzzled his ear.

'What are you going to name her, son?' called
Mrs J from the porch.

'Destiny,' said Jess. 'Because she was always
meant to be mine.' He sprang lightly on to the
mare's bare, gleaming back.

'Need a job, cowboy?' called Ramrod, as he and
the other cowhands rode in off the range. 'Dollar a
day and your keep?'

Jess tightened the new red bandanna round his
throat and straightened his hat. 'Reckon I'm your
man,' he said.

3
Sweet Rain

The first job Jess Ford was given, after he became a cowboy, was to fetch back Bossman J's stolen horses from Indian country. Red-neck Pete had hidden them in Blind Canyon, on the edge of Sioux country, a day's ride from Sundown.

'It could be dangerous, boy,' said Bossman J. 'If you don't want to go, just say the word.'

'I'd like to, sir,' said Jess. 'I've never seen Sioux country.'

'Well if you see any Sioux, you just turn tail and run, lad. I can't spare a good hand like you – not even to git my horses back. Are you sure you know the way?'

'Due north till I hit Squash River, then follow the river upstream to Blind Canyon.'

And that is what Jess did.

★ ★ ★

Squash River carved its way through candy-stripe rock the colour of honey and chocolate. Here and there the rushing water slowed into deep pools, then rattled on again over pebbly shallows. On the far side of the canyon began Sioux land. Blind Canyon was the end of the cattle range.

It took Jess three hours of searching the canyon before he found the horses, but there they were, penned up in a dark cranny of rock. Red-neck Pete had blocked off the open end with a pile of chopped-down cottonwood trees to make a kind of corral.

'Call to them, Destiny. Tell them they're going home,' said Jess, and his horse tossed her head and hinnied softly to the stolen herd. Jess got down and began to pull the cottonwood branches aside. It was mighty hot work.

All of a sudden he thought he heard thunder. Then he looked round and realised it was the noise of galloping hooves echoing off the sides of the ravine. A pinto pony was riding towards him, full tilt, across the river, pebbles and spray flying from under its front feet. The warrior astride its bare back had a splash of warpaint for a face, and long plaits, snaking. The plaits were tipped with steel-grey feathers. War whoops set Jess's hair lifting. And in the Indian's upraised hand was – what? – an arrow? A knife? A tomahawk?

The cowboy jumped backwards, caught his spur in a cottonwood bush and fell back into another. Helplessly entangled, his hat was over his eyes, his ears full of the noise of hooves. Something struck him on the chest. He clutched it in his fist as he got up. The rider had grabbed Destiny's reins and was making off with her, hauling the bit halfway out of her mouth, towing her away. There was a hole scoured in the ground where the pinto pony had stopped and turned in one smooth movement. What riding! Jess could not help but give a whistle of admiration.

He stared for a moment at the broken stick in his hand. Then he purposely gave a much louder whistle. 'It's worth a try,' he told himself.

His horse threw up her head at the familiar

sound of Jess's whistle. Instead of trailing behind the pinto pony, Destiny put in a burst of speed. As they crossed the river, she turned across the path of the pinto, and forced it to swerve wildly. The pony slipped in the wet, and went down. The rider was pitched a great way, hitting some big, stepping-stone rocks and somersaulting over them into a deep-water pool. There was an almighty splash – then silence.

Jess fought off the snagging cottonwood and ran. He splashed through the shallows and clambered on to the highest of the big rocks. The pool beyond was still rippling from the splash. There was no sign of the rider.

May be hiding – keeping down – planning to come at me out of the water, he thought.

Then the pool exploded into spray! Jess saw a pair of arms, a head, a gasping mouth . . . before the drowning warrior sank underwater again.

Jess pulled off his boots, waistcoat, trousers and threw them on to the bank. He dived as deep as he dared, hoping no rocks were jutting out below the surface.

It was cold, cold and dark. The only sound was the roar of bubbles past his ears. He opened his eyes wide, but could see nothing. When his breath was all gone, and he came up for air, the sun felt so good, and the air tasted so fine. A single grey feather, floating on the water, stuck itself to his cheek.

Jess turned turtle and swam down again. A big trout passed right by his face. A beauty! He could not help but make a grab for it. The fish gave one flick of its tail and got away, but Jess's fist closed round something else instead – a rope of dark, plaited hair.

He tugged the Indian to the surface by both plaits, kicking out like a frog. It was a fearful weight to raise, all that sodden doeskin. But as he cupped one hand round a cold face and swam for the rocks, he realised that the wet clothing probably weighed more than the person inside it.

The warpaint was all washed off. There was no mistaking it. His attacker was a girl!

* * *

'I'm dead! Am I dead?' the girl said as she opened her eyes.

'Nope. I pulled you out.'

'Why? I stole your horse.'

'You *tried*. But if Destiny don't choose to go, nobody steals Destiny.'

She looked disappointed, then raised herself on one elbow and said defiantly, 'Still, I counted coup on you!'

'Did what?'

'I touched you with the coup stick. I counted coup on you. I proved my bravery. I thought you'd shoot me, but I did it!'

'I don't have a gun,' said Jess, and her face fell so far that he was almost sorry to have said it. 'Still, you didn't know that. So yes, I reckon you were pretty brave. And you sure can ride a horse.' She beamed at him, a smile like a flash of lightning.

They looked across to where their horses were drinking together at the water's edge. The pinto's nose brushed up against Destiny's.

'What's your name?' asked Jess.

'They call me Sweet Rain.'

'How come you talk English so good?'

'My ma was taken prisoner by the Lakota.'

'The Sioux, you mean. That's terrible!'

Sweet Rain flared her broad Sioux nose at him. 'I mean the Lakota. Only ignorant enemies call us just 'Sioux'. I'm proud to be Lakota! My pa was Lakota!'

'And you want him to be proud of you?'

Sweet Rain shrugged. 'Pa and Ma's dead. Now I don't . . . fit in, back at the village. I'm not Lakota; I'm not white. If I was a boy, I could prove myself – go hunting, go on the warpath . . .'

'Touch a white man with your coup stick,' said Jess. Sweet Rain blushed. 'Come back with me, then. You'd fit in fine in Sundown.' He was not quite sure it was true, but he said it anyway.

'Huh!' Sweet Rain sprang to her feet, stamping fiercely. 'I hate all white men. All of you! You come here, shoot our buffalo and . . .'

But she had stood up too quickly. She was half full of river water, and dizzy. Jess jumped up and caught her in his arms before she fainted. She struggled and punched at him. '*I* found all those horses! No one else knows about them! I was going to take them home! Imagine! Coming home with twenty saddle horses! But oh no, you come along – a boy . . .'

'They belong to my boss!' Jess protested. 'They were stolen. A horse thief hid them here. I have to take them back. I just have to. It's my first job!'

A shout echoed down the ravine.

Two Lakota braves stood on the skyline – no mistaking these for girls. Each held a bow at full stretch.

And their arrows were pointing at Jess.

'My cousins. They think you are trying to take me prisoner,' whispered Sweet Rain.

Jess looked down at his long-johns and bare feet, and groaned. 'I'd've liked to die with my boots on,' he confessed.

Suddenly Sweet Rain moved round in front of him and stood, arms out, like a star, shielding Jess from the arrows. She called out to the young men in Sioux, but he understood well enough what she was saying:

'*He saved my life! I was drowning and he saved me!*'

The warriors came closer, their bowstrings at half-stretch, their eyes watching, watching.

'Lakota land,' said one.

'Don't tell them about the horses!' whispered Sweet Rain. '*They* will take them, and *I* found them first.'

Jess did not want to tell the young men about Bossman J's horses, either. So he called back, 'Fishing! I was fishing!'

'I see no fish. You catch Sweet Rain, yes? You catch sister Sweet Rain.'

Sweet Rain was indignant. 'He didn't catch me! I counted coup on him! I did!'

The braves looked at one another and sniggered. Their sniggers grew into a roar of laughter. '*You?* Count coup? Huh! White tongue in you lies. She lies, eh, pale-face?' Sweet Rain bit her lip and gave a small sob of misery.

'No,' said Jess after a moment's pause. 'She does not lie. She hit me with a stick. She broke her stick on me. She came at me so fast, I . . . I did not even have time to draw a gun. Only Sioux can ride that well. You must be proud to have such a sister.'

Their mouths fell open. They gaped at Sweet Rain, as though they had never properly seen her before.

'We have spoken words of peace now,' Jess went on. 'She spared my life, and I spared hers. We are even.' He held Sweet Rain's hand as she balanced across the wet rocks, and he helped her on to her horse. Then she rode along the canyon past her cousins, her wet moccasins rapping on the pinto's flanks, her long plaits dripping, her head held high. The warriors followed after her, speechless with disbelief. They did not know what else to do: if their cousin had made peace with this white man, then they must not break it. From the end of the valley all three turned and watched for Jess to leave.

There was nothing else he *could* do but leave. Hopping into his trousers, struggling into his boots, he clambered on to Destiny's back and rode out of there, fast. He could feel Lakota eyes watching him all the way out of Blind Canyon. In fact, he cleared out of there as quick as he knew how, before they changed their minds about letting him go in peace. Let Sweet Rain have the stolen horses, he thought. Indians might throw their lives away trying to capture horses, but Jess had too many other things planned for *his* life.

No sooner was he back on the range than the sun went down. But Jess rode on, taking his direction from the stars. He was too scared to make camp and light a fire which the Lakota would surely see. Towards dawn, though, he saw the friendly orange glow of some other cowboy campfire. Obadiah Thorn, one of the other Lazy J ranch hands, was sleeping out on the range.

Jess took a deep breath and let it go in a sigh. He could not put it off any longer. He would have to admit to leaving those horses behind. Obadiah would laugh at him. Obadiah would say, 'The boss should never have sent a boy on a man's job.'

Obadiah Thorn rolled out of his blanket, rifle at the ready, and bleared at Jess through the darkness. 'Who's there? Ah, it's you, boy! So, you didn't find the horses, then?'

'Well—'

'Not your fault, son. 'Spect them injuns found 'em before you. They'll be riding 'em round Sioux country by now.'

'I did find them,' said Jess gloomily, warming his hands at the fire.

'Couldn't you handle them, boy? Twenty skittish critters – they can take some handling. You shoulda taken me along with you.'

'I . . .' Jess could not think how to say what had happened. 'I ran into some injun trouble,' he said.

'Ah! And there's you without a gun.' Obadiah poured him a cup of coffee from the pot balanced over the fire, and waited for Jess to tell him the whole story. But Jess just stared into the fire, his cheeks turning red. An hour passed. Maybe more. Obadiah tried to get in some more sleep. The eastern sky was starting to glow like a hot wire.

Suddenly, through the half-light came the drumming of hooves. Obadiah wriggled out of his blanket again. 'It's a herd of buffalo set to trample us!'

But it was not buffalo. It was a string of twenty saddle horses being led by a single rider. Sweet Rain. The pinto's patches of white shone in the darkness. Destiny called out softly to him.

'I brought you your hat,' said Sweet Rain. 'You left it among the cottonwood.'

Jess took it from her, patting the pinto's neck. 'Thank you.'

'I brought you your horses, too,' she said. 'Now your boss will not be angry with you.'

'But what about you . . . ?' Jess began.

'I don't need them. I won great honour counting coup on the enemy. They would never have taken my word, back at the village. But now they have to. They heard it from the lips of a white man.' She reached down and took his hat back for a moment, pulled a feather from the end of one plait and stuck it into the hatband. 'I said before . . .' she began shyly. 'I said I hated all white men.' She put the hat on his head. 'But maybe not all.'

'Good,' said Jess. 'A cowboy needs a friend. See you around, Sweet Rain.'

'Well, I'll be corn-shucked and eaten sweet!' exclaimed Obadiah, as Sweet Rain rode off. 'How in tarnation did a scrap of a girl like that fetch twenty skittish horses all this way in the dark?'

'Ah!' said Jess mysteriously. 'She's quite a girl.'

Dawn made a pale line around the rim of the sky – as if the night were raising its hat to a lady.

'Go in peace, Sweet Rain,' said Jess under his breath. 'And come back soon.'

4

The Noon Stage

All Sundown turned out to meet the noonday stagecoach. It came every Wednesday and Saturday. Sometimes there were letters aboard, and sometimes parcels. There were newspapers from back East, and bolts of cloth, maybe even banknotes for the bank. Some days passengers got out for lunch and a wash, before continuing their journey. But today, today there would be someone getting off the noon stage who was planning to stay.

A doctor was arriving. Sundown had never had a doctor before. Until now, if folks got ill, either they died or they got better. But now Doctor Luke was coming.

The Mayor had put an advert in the *Eastern News*:

///

WANTED
Town Doctor, Sundown, Paradise County.
Plenty of Trade.

///

And Doctor Luke had answered it. He was young
– only just out of college – but the Mayor said that
any doctor was better than no doctor at all. His
surgery was all ready for him, right next door to the
funeral parlour. Everyone in Sundown had given a
dollar or a pot of paint to make it nice. And Widow
Bramley said he could live in her back room until
he got a place of his own.

The girls were already practising fainting. The
old folks grumbled, 'Never needed doctors when
we was young.' The Mayor's wife was making a
long list of all her illnesses. But everyone was there,
waiting to see the new doctor, waiting for the noon
stage. It was never late.

Noon came, but the stagecoach did not.

'Maybe there's bad weather down the road,'
said the Mayor.

'Maybe one of the horses cast a shoe,' said Widow Bramley.

'Maybe the doctor was busy curing someone, and they waited for him,' said Jess Ford.

'The noon stage waits for no one,' said the Sheriff darkly. Nobody dared say what they were really thinking: *what if the stage had run into bad trouble?*

One o'clock came, and the old folk went to sit down in the shade. The children got bored and ran off.

'Outlaws?' said Ben Block.

'Injuns?' said Obadiah Thorn.

'An accident, maybe,' said the funeral director.

Then the banker suddenly blurted out: 'I have money coming in on that stage! A whole shipment of new coins. What if someone found out . . . ?'

'Well, we ain't gonna solve the mystery standing here,' said the Sheriff. 'I'll ride down the track and take a look.'

'Jess Ford's already gone,' said Belle from the Silver Dollar Saloon. 'He rode off on Destiny a while back.'

* * *

The track stretched away across the range, empty. There was no sign of the stagecoach. Destiny's galloping strides ate up mile upon mile, and soon Jess reached that patch of desert which laps down into Paradise County like a great yellow tongue. Huge rocks loomed up, and cactus bushes and termite hills. But there was no sign of the noon stage.

Jess poured some water into his hat and gave Destiny a drink. He wished he were with his new friend Sweet Rain. She was teaching him to track like a wolverine and think like a cougar. But today he was on his own and had to rely on his ordinary human instincts. 'We'll go as far as Coney Creek, then turn back,' he said.

Ten minutes later, ahead of him on the track, Jess saw a barefoot man in a flat black hat, picking his way painfully over the hot, stony ground. A black coat hung over one arm, and a bootlace tie hung loose at his throat.

'Doctor Luke?' said Jess, reining in.

'How did you know? Yes! The stage! It was held up! Two villains with bandannas over their faces! Seems there was money aboard . . . Who are you?'

'Jess Ford's the name. From Sundown. When

the stage was late, I came looking for you.'

'Thanks. I was walking back to the last town we passed through – to get help. But they took my boots to slow me down.'

'Where's Willie, the driver?' asked Jess.

'They needed him to drive the stage.'

'They stole the whole stagecoach? Willie and all?'

'There was too much money for them to carry away in their saddle bags,' explained the doctor.

There was nothing to see but desert for ten miles. 'Get up behind me,' said Jess, 'and we'll go after them.'

'Go after them? Two of us? On one horse?'

'I think we should. Willie may need help. He isn't as young as he was. What do you say?'

Doctor Luke looked at the sky with one eye and pursed his lips. 'I say let's go. I left my bag in the stage, and what good is a doctor without his bag?'

So Doctor Luke climbed up behind Jess, and they backtracked to where the stage had been held up. The tracks left by the stagecoach showed which way the robbers had gone. Jess rode between the wheel marks, hoping no gust of wind would rub them out. They rode towards the skyline, alone in the desert but for snakes and coney rabbits. A handful of vultures circled in the sky, like pieces of paper blowing about.

The doctor cleared his throat politely. 'What exactly do you plan on doing, once we catch up?' he asked.

'Reckon I'll figure that out when we do.'

'You won't go shooting anybody, will you?'

'That would be difficult,' said Jess with a grin. 'I don't have a gun.'

'I'm glad about that,' said the doctor. 'I think.'

Even with two riders on her back, Destiny covered the ground magnificently – faster than any stagecoach could go.

'Remind me to buy a horse like this, if I ever reach Sundown,' said Doctor Luke.

'There *isn't* another horse like Destiny,' said Jess proudly. He got off and lay down on the ground. He pressed his ear to the earth and listened. 'Sweet Rain taught me how to do this. She's a Lakota friend of mine. Yep. I reckon we're catching up with them pretty fast. It's not easy to drive a stage over the desert.'

★ ★ ★

One bandit was sitting up beside Willie, on the stagecoach. The other was riding alongside, leading the spare horse. Looking back, they saw a plume of dust behind them and did not realise it was only one horse.

'There's a posse after us, Marnie!' said one.

'We could outrun them, Barney,' said the other, 'if only these nags weren't so lazy!' And he fired his gun to frighten the coach-horses into pulling harder.

He succeeded. The team of four rolled their eyes in terror, then bolted. Willie tried to steady them, but they just took off, careering over soft dirt and hard rocks. At last a front wheel struck a big boulder and shattered. Even so, Willie might have saved the coach from disaster: he was an excellent driver. But the robber beside him snatched the reins in panic. He hauled on them so hard that they broke. The shipment of coins stowed under the floor made the coach extra heavy. It slewed sideways; two wheels came clear off the ground.

The traces snapped and the harness, too. As the pulling-horses broke loose, the stage turned over once, twice, three times. The bandit on horseback saw the coach rolling towards him like the end of the world. Willie was thrown clear, but the two bandits were pinned under the wagon. A shower of dollars and cents dropped on them out of the smashed floor of the stagecoach.

★ ★ ★

The dust had not even settled when Jess and Doctor Luke arrived on the scene. The coach lay on its side, propped a little way off the ground by its open door. But half of it stuck out alarmingly over thin air: the chase had brought them to the very brink of a steep sandstone cliff. At any moment it might slither over the edge to destruction.

'Are you hurt bad, Willie?' Jess asked as he brought Destiny to a halt in a cloud of dust.

'Just my leg,' said Willie. 'Are my horses okay?'

'They're fine,' said Jess. 'I brought a doctor to fix your leg. You're privileged. You can be Doctor Luke's very first patient.'

As Willie got over his fright, he became more his old self. 'No one told me I was carrying bank money,' he complained grumpily. 'I thought the coach weighed heavy today, but no one said to me, *Willie, there's a ton of coins in the bottom of your wagon; watch out for bandits.'*

'Where are the bandits, Willie?' asked Doctor Luke, binding a splint to the broken leg.

'Under the wagon,' said Willie. 'Eating dirt like they deserve.'

Doctor Luke ran to the stagecoach. The wheels were still spinning. Pinned under it were two men – each with a clean starched bandanna over his face. The bandannas flickered a little. 'They're still breathing!' called the doctor. 'Help me get them out, Jess!'

'Leave 'em. Good riddance, I say.' That was Willie's opinion.

'Guess they learned a lesson today,' said Jess. 'Won't make a habit of holding up stagecoaches, not after this, I reckon.' And he went to help.

Luke was trying to find a way in to the men – through the windows, under the wheels. 'Keep out of there, doc!' warned Jess. 'If that stage topples over, it'll take you and them with it over the edge!'

He whistled to Destiny, and when she came trotting up, took the coiled lasso off his saddle. He tied one end to the pommel, the other to the window bar of the stage. 'Now, don't let it fall on me, girl!' he told his horse. She took the strain, while Jess squeezed under the coach.

'Why you and not me?' asked Luke, as Jess squirmed out of sight.

The answer came back from under the wreck. 'Sundown's got plenty of cowboys, but it doesn't have one doctor. I could never hold my head up in town if I'd let you get yourself flattened by the noon stage.'

Dollars and cents rained down on Jess out of the hidden compartment in the floor. He put on his hat again to protect his head from them. The broken door groaned under the weight of the wagon. At any moment it might give way. Then the stage would slide over the brink of the cliff, carrying Jess and the bandits with it, and dragging Destiny off her feet. Jess gouged away with his bare hands at the stones and sand – like a rabbit digging under a fence. He had to work curled up awkwardly in the small space. When he found the doctor's boots and black medical bag, he pushed them clear of the wreck. Then he went on digging carefully round the trapped men. One bandit was unconscious. The other was whimpering sorrowfully.

'How d'you know about the money?' he asked.

'We were cashiers at the bank, back East,' groaned Marnie. 'Thought it could be easy! But we never saw the Wild West before.'

'I'd stick to counting out other people's money in future,' said Jess.

He wriggled outside and pulled Barney by the ankles, dragging him clear of the wreck. Then he went back in for the other one. As he pulled Marnie out, the door hinges snapped with a noise like a pistol shot. Destiny gave a shrill cry and leaned back on her haunches. But the great weight of the stagecoach was just too much for her, and she began to skid on her hocks.

Jess pulled out his knife and sawed at the rope. Strand by strand it broke, but still the stage was dragging Destiny off her feet. Finally the rope gave way. Destiny sat back on her haunches, and the stagecoach tumbled over the edge, sliding and rolling to the very bottom of the steep slope, where it settled and sagged on three splayed wheels.

Three more seconds and Jess's horse would have gone with it.

★ ★ ★

Almost everybody had gone to bed when the noon stage rolled into Sundown at midnight. But the Mayor, the Sheriff and Widow Bramley all came out to give the doctor a proper welcome. The banker came running, wanting to know what had become of his coins. In nightshirts and overcoats they gathered in front of the brightly lit Silver Dollar Saloon to get their first glimpse of Doctor Luke. Belle the singer came out on to the saloon balcony, brushing her hair.

They could hardly believe their eyes when they saw the stage. It sagged along like a sackful of kindling, one door gone and broken planks of wood sticking out all over. One wheel was missing. It looked like it had been to the moon and back. Jess Ford the cowboy was trotting behind the battered coach on his lovely black mare.

The Mayor threw open the remaining door. It came off its hinges and dropped at his feet, but the Mayor was not to be put off making his speech of welcome:

'May I just say, Doctor Luke, how glad we are in this little town of ours . . . *Jehosofat!*' Inside, three men, bandaged, splinted and propped up on cushions, glared back at him. One of them was

Willie the driver. The other two had their hands tied with rope. 'Which one is Luke?' asked the Mayor, bewildered.

'I am,' said the man perched up on the driver's box. 'I brought a couple of patients with me, in case you folk were all too healthy.'

★ ★ ★

But there was no chance of that. Next day, when word got about that Doctor Luke had rescued Willie and the noon stage, everyone wanted to meet him. So they were suddenly took bad with a sore throat, a banged thumb, a case of jitters or a cold in the elbow. Some even brought their livestock for a cure from the new doctor. Widow Bramley served griddle cakes on the porch, saying, ' My doctor will see you just as soon as he can.'

But Jess Ford, meanwhile, had gone back to the Lazy J Ranch. He was up with the sun, roping steers. When he came to put his hat on, he found the lining stuffed with dollars and cents from the wreck of the stage.

Jess sewed the money into his mattress. Right now, life was good, working on the Lazy J. But a cowboy needs savings against the time he is laid up sick, or the day he takes a ride along the Lonesome Trail, in search of adventure.

5

The Army Brand

Jess and Destiny were quite a team. At round-up time, the black mare wove nimbly in and out of the cattle, cantering so smoothly that roping was easy.

'Hold it there, lady,' Jess would say, and Destiny stopped instantly. 'Pull tight,' Jess would say, and Destiny walked backwards until the rope went taut and the steer toppled to the ground, kicking. 'Ride 'em in,' Jess would say, and Destiny would prance sideways, driving strays back towards the main herd. She was dainty as a ballet dancer, and as strong as a railroad engine.

Jess and Sweet Rain were quite a team, as well,

though no one else knew it. Since their first adventure, they had met lots of times out on the range. At first they thought it was by accident. Then they realised it was because they liked one another, got on well. There were people in Sundown and at the Lazy J who would not have approved of Jess fishing, boating, riding around with a Sioux maiden. They would have called her an injun squaw and seen no farther than her headband and braids. But Jess and Sweet Rain – their horses too, come to that – had been born on the range. They liked the feel of the same wind and what it did to rocks. They liked the same sunsets, the same star patterns, the same moon. And they liked each other – raising a hand in distant greeting, like the tall, glove-shaped mitten rocks which hail each other across the wide open spaces.

One fine day, the ranch hands at the Lazy J stopped work to watch a cloud of dust travel over the range towards them. Gradually they picked out the blue of uniforms – 'Cavalry soldiers,' said Ben Block – and the string of riderless horses trotting behind.

'Buying horses for the army, I reckon,' said Bossman J. He was pleased. The army paid a good price for horses, and he had a dozen nice colts and fillies for sale in the long paddock. 'Fill the trough for the horses, Jess,' he said, 'then put some coffee on for the troops.'

So Jess hitched Destiny to the paddock rail and pumped water into the long horse trough. The cavalry troopers rode, single file, into the yard, dismounted and left their horses by the trough. They were bays and roans mostly, with a couple of black colts. The army liked their horses dark or drab – to blend in with the landscape when the enemy was about.

Jess stroked the army horses and wondered what made a man join the cavalry when he could be a cowboy instead. Adventure, perhaps. Or excitement? Or free boots? He stroked the young horses newly bought for army service, and fingered the army brand burned into their hides. 'Poor beasts,' he murmured. 'No one asked *you* if you wanted to join the army.' Already there was a brazier lit in the yard. The army farrier was heating a branding iron, ready to brand any horses bought from the Lazy J.

When Jess went back to his horse, the officer in charge was standing beside Destiny, patting her neck and talking to the rancher; there was an odd look on Bossman J's face. 'Captain Morgan likes your horse, Jess,' he said.

'She's the best,' said Jess proudly.

'I'd like to buy her,' said the Captain. He was a dark, dapper man with a sharp jaw underlined with a sharp black beard.

'Who wouldn't?' said Jess.

'I'd pay a good price,' said the Captain.

'Thanks, but she's not for sale – not at any price,' said Jess.

Slowly, Captain Morgan pulled off his black gloves, finger by finger, as if pulling the legs off two black spiders. 'I don't think you understand me, laddie. I am requisitioning this horse for the army.'

'What does he mean, boss?' said Jess. 'What does "requisition" mean? He's going to take my horse? He can't take my horse, sir, can he? Can he?'

'The government needs good horses, son . . .' began Bossman J, his neck turning red.

'And my orders are to get them, laddie,' said Captain Morgan in his sharp-clipped voice. 'I always obey orders. Take your tack off the mare, then come and get your money. You can soon buy yourself another horse. Call it your patriotic duty.'

Jess felt as if he had just stepped out in front of a train and it had run clear over him. He could not move. He could not think. He stood by Destiny's head. He could see his pale, shocked face reflected in her brown eyes.

There was a smell of hot metal and burning hair. Destiny jumped suddenly sideways with a shrill cry. The farrier stood there, holding the branding iron to her skin.

'No!' cried Jess, but it was too late. The army brand smoked on Destiny's flank. 'Why?' he asked helplessly.

'The Captain wants this one for himself,' said the farrier. 'He knows a good horse when he sees one. And once he makes up his mind to have something, the Captain never lets anyone stand in his way. I'm sorry, kid.'

Inside the house, the Captain gave Jess a paper to sign and thirty dollars. 'Put a cross if you don't know how to write your name, laddie.'

Jess wrote, *Jess Ford – Robbed* in his beautiful handwriting. Then he ran to the bunkhouse and slammed the huge doors with a deafening crash.

The Captain, his men and the newly bought horses spent the night at the local army fort – Fort Paradise. Major Bull, who ran Fort Paradise, was startled by the arrival of such a crowd, and ran about in a panic, organising beds for the troop to sleep in and meals for them to eat.

After a sleepless night, Jess borrowed a horse and rode over to the fort at first light. He did not know why, exactly, but he knew he had to go, to be near his horse.

His friend Sweet Rain the Lakota was there already, sitting on the steps of the trading post, waiting for it to open. She had two handsome woven blankets to sell there. When she heard about Destiny, she tossed her head so furiously that her long plaits flew. 'If this man has stolen your horse, you must steal her back!'

Jess shook his head sadly. 'Stealing from the army, that's a hanging crime. Anyways, if Captain Morgan lost Destiny now, he'd know exactly who to blame. He would just come looking for me and take her back.' They sat on the steps, too miserable to talk. Sweet Rain's pinto pony hung his head as if he too were grieving for Destiny.

The fort bugler sounded Reveille, to get the soldiers out of their beds. Then he sounded Boots and Saddles: Major Bull was going to let the visiting Captain take morning inspection. It seemed the hospitable thing to do.

Out came the foot soldiers, banging their boots in the dust, buttoning their jackets. Out came the cavalrymen, leading their horses at the trot. Out came Major Bull in his best uniform (though his braces were hanging down at the back).

Out came Captain Morgan, as smart and thin as a viper. Out came Destiny in army tack, brushed and gleaming, led by a groom who gave the reins to the Captain. And Captain Morgan mounted up on Jess's horse, haughty and tall, ready to inspect the garrison.

'I can't bear to look,' said Jess.

'Oh, I think you should,' said Sweet Rain.

Destiny went as stiff as a rocking horse carved in wood. Her legs were rigid, her flanks quivering. She tossed her head and snuffed the air. Her eyes rolled menacingly. Suddenly she dipped her head and arched her back. And Captain Morgan flew through the air and landed on his chest.

One of the foot soldiers sniggered. Major Bull glared at his troops, forbidding them to laugh. Captain Morgan picked himself up and slashed the air with his riding whip, furious, his vanity wounded.

Destiny looked across at Jess and, for the first time, Jess realised: 'She knows I'm here!' He put a finger to his lips. 'Ssh. Gently now, lady. We don't want him to use that whip on you,' he murmured.

Captain Morgan remounted. Jess sauntered over to the edge of the parade ground, his hands in his pockets. One fist was closed round the thirty dollars Morgan had paid him. 'Now. *Pull tight, girl,*' he said under his breath.

Sure enough, Destiny dipped her rump and walked sharply backwards, past the ranks of saluting soldiers.

'Hold it there,' whispered Jess, and she stopped dead. 'Now *ride 'em in,*' hissed Jess, and his trusty roping horse pranced sideways across the parade ground, scattering troopers like skittles. They dived to the right and left, laughing till the buttons flew off their jackets. Then they yelled and skipped aside again as Destiny came prancing back across the parade ground. '*Hold it there, girl!*' And Destiny stopped dead so that the Captain sprawled over her ears to land on his hands and knees in the dust.

Morgan, his face red with fury, pulled his pistol from its holster and pointed it: Jess thought he was going to be shot. 'I suppose you think you're very clever, laddie!'

Jess spread both hands wide, and shrugged

innocently. 'She's a roping horse, sir. She does what she was trained to do.' The soldiers on the parade ground laughed all the harder: they had to lean against each other or fall over. 'You should never have bought her if you didn't want her for roping, sir,' said Jess mildly.

Morgan fired his pistol in the air, and the laughing stopped. 'If you think you can make a fool of me, you're very much mistaken, laddie,' he said dangerously. 'If I can't *ride* her, I'll use her for a pack animal.' He came strutting over, and jutted his sharp beard in Jess's face. 'That horse is army property now, and she obeys my commands, or I'll sell her for meat to the injuns. You hear me, laddie?'

Jess dropped his eyes, let his shoulders sag, and walked away. The coins in his pocket were bruising the inside of his fist. 'It's over,' he said to Sweet Rain. 'I've lost my horse.'

Sweet Rain said nothing, but climbed the steps of the trading post as its doors opened, carrying her two woven blankets. With a heart as heavy as a cannonball, Jess rode back to the Lazy J on his borrowed horse.

★ ★ ★

That night, Captain Morgan camped on the open range. He had a fine big tent, lit by a paraffin lamp. His men slept on the ground, with their saddles for pillows. And the horses, their front feet hobbled with leather straps, chewed grass or slept with the starlight on their backs. A sentry dozed over his rifle, snickering to himself, from time to time, at the thought of Captain Morgan trying to ride the black mare.

Through the grass, worming along on hands and thighs, knife between teeth, a single Lakota warrior approached the grazing horses. Between their restless hooves, beneath their long jaws, the warrior slithered, slicing through the leather hobbles as though they were bootlaces . . .

An owl hooted. A coyote yelped. The sentry started out of sleep. This was not coyote country! He reached for his rifle. It was gone! In the same second, he heard a shot ring out.

All the horses threw up their heads and bolted.

The shadow of Captain Morgan lurched upright in the lit tent. He knocked his head on the paraffin lamp and set it swinging. Then the stampeding horses demolished the tent round about him. They stepped smartly over their riders and saddles before jostling away into the darkness. The sentry was jumping up and down and yelling, *'Attack! We're under attack! Injuns attacking!'*

By morning's light, they found several feathers, a scattering of beads and some fringing from an Indian tunic. So it must have been Indians, mustn't it?

'There were dozens of them,' the sentry vowed. 'A whole raiding party!'

Captain Morgan ground his teeth and kicked the ruins of his tent. 'And couldn't we have shot just one of them?'

'The horses!' his men protested. 'They came right at us!'

Later they managed to round up most of the horses. Only the black mare was lost without trace.

'Good riddance,' said Captain Morgan. 'The brute was worthless anyway.'

'Just wait till those injuns try to ride her, eh, sir?' said the sergeant, with a friendly grin. Morgan silenced him with a look as sour as lemons, and pulled on his black gloves, finger by finger. Inwardly he had vowed never to set foot in Paradise County again.

★ ★ ★

Jess hardly slept all night for missing Destiny. He was first awake in the bunkhouse, put the coffee on the stove, then slid open the big barn doors to go and wash at the trough pump.

As he held his head under the rushing water, he became aware of someone else nearby. A horse was drinking from the other end of the trough: a black mare wearing a woven Indian saddle blanket.

'The blanket hides the army brand,' said Sweet Rain, who was sitting on the paddock fence. 'You will have to use it always.'

'Did you weave it?' asked Jess.

'Yes, I wove it.'

'I'll use it always,' he said. 'Did you steal her?'

'Not by any law of the Lakota Nation,' she replied. 'I took back the horse of a friend. That is all.'

Then Jess fetched his tack from the barn, and he and Sweet Rain went riding together before breakfast, she on her pretty pinto, he on the black mare called Destiny. They made quite a team.

6

The Christmas Mittens

Jess picked out the softest, silkiest pair of fur mittens on sale in the town store, and paid for them with a fistful of dollars. The storekeeper raised her eyebrows in astonishment. 'A Christmas present?' she said.

'Sort of,' said Jess. Around him were piles of tinned food and sacks of meal, tools, bullets and clothes. There were bolts of calico, ferocious knives, pots, pans and brooms. Jess had spent an hour trying to find the perfect present, but in the end he chose the mittens: the best in the shop.

'Of course after the *railroad* comes to town, I shall have a much larger choice,' the storekeeper boasted, as she wrapped the mittens in red paper.

'Yes! Imagine!' exclaimed Jess. 'The railroad!'

There was great excitement in Sundown at the news. The barber told his customers, the men told the ladies, the ladies told the children, the children told each other: 'Have you heard? The railroad's coming to Sundown!'

There were two maps pinned up outside the newspaper office, so everyone could see what was planned. One was a map of the town, showing where the station would be: the sidings, the stockyards, the railroad office. Dirty fingermarks soon made a black smudge over the spot where the trains would pull in.

'I'll get a job as a guard,' said Hobo Hill.

'I'll get a job as a fireman,' said Matt Bunt.

'I'll get a job as a porter,' said Jemima Coolidge. (She had the muscles for it, too.)

'I'll ride the train out of here one day,' said Ma Stapley's little boy. 'And go to the big city, and be president.'

The other map showed Paradise County. Two dotted lines ran across it, straight as rulers. The railroad had not yet decided which route the line would take after Sundown. Route B went through the desert by the way of Coney Creek. Route A went across the Squash River and straight on.

'But that's Lakota territory,' said Jess out loud.

'That won't worry the railroad company,' said Pat Bodger cheerfully. 'They've plenty of lines through injun country.'

'But what . . .'

'If the injuns don't like it, the army jest drive 'em out!'

Jess backed off the sidewalk and mounted his horse. Suddenly he did not feel so very thrilled about the railroad coming to town. He rode directly out to Mitten Rock and left his hat there, pinned down with a rock. That was the sign agreed with Sweet Rain, the sign that meant, 'Let's talk.'

Sure enough, two days later, she appeared out of nowhere. He was driving young cattle in closer to the ranch, because there was snow in the air. And Sweet Rain just rode up, wearing his hat. She gave it back. 'You want to see me?' she said.

She was wearing a thick doeskin dress, long boots and a blanket clutched over her hair and shoulders. But Jess could see that the fist holding the blanket was purple with cold. He was really pleased he had chosen the mittens. He pulled the red paper packet out of his saddlebag. 'A Christmas present.'

'We don't keep Christmas,' she said.

'No,' said Jess. 'But I do. Anyway, I never thanked you properly for getting Destiny back from the army.'

When she saw the mittens, she did not hide her delight. 'They're wonderful! Warm and wonderful! Thank you!'

'But I have some bad news, too . . .'

He did not want to tell her about the railroad. He did not even want to think about that great steel track ploughing through this hunting ground, that fishing place, those burial grounds sacred to Sweet Rain and the other Lakota. But he did tell her.

Her cold face grew even paler than before. Pale and hard. 'You white men. You won't rest till you drive us off our fathers' lands.'

'Not me! I don't want it! I'm determined they won't build that way. Believe me! I'll find a way to stop them!'

Sweet Rain looked down at the mittens, and began to pull them off.

'Don't,' said Jess. 'Not yet! Give me a chance. If I can't stop them, you can give back the mittens. Next spring. Deal?'

'I must go and tell this news to the tribe,' was all she said. Clutching the blanket tight around her face with a gloved hand, she turned her back on Jess and rode away.

All through Christmas, Jess tried to think of a way to make the railroad choose the other, desert route. He could argue with them, but he knew he would lose. He could start up a campaign, but he knew just how many people in Sundown were so afraid of the Sioux as to gladly see them driven off their land. No, he would have to tackle the problem some other way.

There were pies and punch and puddings at the ranch house. There was snow on the range. There were carols at the church, and all the cowboys sang the Cowboys' Hymn. But as Jess sat there, in the Christmas candlelight, all he could think of was those railroad engines in their sheds. They were waiting, like black monsters in their lairs, to hurtle across the countryside and ravage Lakota territory.

Doctor Luke was late for the carol service. He squeezed in beside Jess, apologising. 'The Gomez child has a fever. I had to pay her a visit.'

Quite suddenly, the pew was half empty, as the ladies on the far side of Doctor Luke all huddled away from him, like chickens from a fox. 'Never fear, ladies,' he soothed them. 'It was nothing catching.' He winked at Jess. 'If I'd said it was smallpox, I could have emptied the church in ten seconds, you know . . . Are you all right, Jess?'

'Yes,' said Jess decidedly. '*Yes, yes, yes, yes, yes!* At least I will be, if you'll help me!'

'Shshshsh!' said the ladies fiercely. The choir was starting to sing.

★ ★ ★

The first good weather brought the railroad's chief surveyor to Sundown. He wanted a guide to the local countryside, and Jess volunteered at once. But the Sheriff swore in a couple of armed deputies as well, 'in case those Sioux make trouble'.

'They're no danger right now,' said Jess mysteriously.

They rode out a far as the Squash River. The melting snows had turned it into a rushing torrent.

'*That's* no problem,' said the Surveyor with a confident sneer. 'I've built bridges over far bigger rivers.'

They rode between the striped rocks of the

Blind Canyon. '*This* is no problem,' said the Surveyor with a haughty sniff. 'I've built bridges over canyons twice as wide.'

'But isn't the desert route easier?' asked Jess eagerly.

'Steam engines need water, sonny,' said the Surveyor, as if to a little child. 'And railroad tracks don't rest happily on sand.'

So on they rode, through the pretty Lakota countryside, and though the deputies kept a lookout all the while, they did not see a single soul. Not one.

'That's the Lakota burial ground,' Jess pointed out. 'This is where their shamans have visions. These trees are where the young men cut the wood for their bows.'

'Good,' said the Surveyor grimly. 'When we rip it out, they may move on. Passengers don't like injuns living alongside the track. We like to shift them if we can.'

The deputies nodded, in agreement, and Jess could feel his temper growing like a fire inside him. He took several deep breaths and kept silent.

Still no Lakota showed themselves. It was as if the countryside was already deserted. Then Sweet Rain's village came in sight. It lay right in the path of the proposed railroad.

'You won't want to go any closer,' said Jess.

'What's those pieces of yellow cloth hung up in the trees?' said Deputy Hobo.

'A warning to strangers,' said Jess.

'And what's that smell?' said Deputy Matt.

'They're burning herbs to keep off disease,' said Jess.

'But where in the blue blazes is everyone?' Hobo burst out at last. At any moment, he expected savage Lakota to leap out of the trees and ambush him.

'All inside their tents, of course,' said Jess casually. 'Either they're sick, or they're looking after the sick. Myself, I think I'll ride round, if it's all the same with you, gentlemen. I don't care to get too close to smallpox.'

'SMALLPOX?'

The Surveyor dropped his theodolite. Deputy Hobo pulled his bandanna up over his nose. Deputy Matt turned his horse round then and there. The wind blowing up from the village brought the faint sound of groaning and sobbing.

★ ★ ★

'But are you *certain* it's smallpox?' the Surveyor asked Jess a fifth time, as they galloped back across the Squash River ford.

'You'd have to ask Doctor Luke in town,' said Jess. 'It might only be measles. Or typhus.'

So the Surveyor asked Sundown's town doctor if he knew what ailed the tribe up beyond the Squash River.

Doctor Luke snatched a white gauze mask out of the drawer of his desk and put it on. Only his eyes frowned back at the Surveyor. 'Well, smallpox, of course! The land out there is riddled with it. The trees, the river. The land where they bury their dead, of course. But most anywhere they've set down. Their sheep, too, naturally. Their horses . . . Fortunately the Sioux don't come to the likes of me for doctoring. And if you have been in contact with them, gentlemen, I fear I *may* have to place you in quarantine for a few weeks . . .'

He turned his blue eyes on Jess and one of them flickered shut – almost as if he were winking.

⋆ ⋆ ⋆

An excited crowd of Sundowners pressed around

the Surveyor at the bar of the Silver Dollar Saloon, to see what this clever man from back East had decided about the future of their town.

'Simple, yes,' the Surveyor was saying grandly. 'I've built railroads over deserts *far* dryer than that one. That's why I've decided on Route B – through the desert and past Coney Creek . . .'

Jess took off his hat to wipe his brow with relief. He looked at the battered old hat: he must go and post it at Mitten Rock, as a signal to Sweet Rain that the plan had worked. He wanted to see her, too. He wanted to congratulate her on the show. Fancy her being able to persuade the whole tribe to join in the charade!

He tried to imagine them all crouching inside their tents, peeping out through the seams, groaning and grinning and watching for the Enemy to hurry away. It made Jess smile himself to think of it.

He did leave his hat at Mitten Rock. But no Sweet Rain appeared. After a week, he said to his horse, 'I'd best get out there again, Destiny. Maybe my hat blew away.' But he was half afraid, as he rode Destiny out towards the strange wind-carved, hand-shaped landmark, that he might find his hat still in place, and the fur mittens beside them that he had given her for Christmas. Perhaps he was just too much of a white man to keep the friendship of a Lakota maiden.

But when he got to the rock, Sweet Rain had not returned his gloves. She had simply answered his gift with a Christmas present of her own. At least the children of her tribe had done.

For Mitten Rock was painted with a hundred colourful figures, animals, stars, patterns, handprints, flowers . . . All around the base, as high as the tallest child could reach, the rock was decorated. Jess thought it was the best Christmas present he had ever received.

Even if the month was March, and the grass on the range was already bright with spring flowers.